T0193472

ROAD MAKER ONE
and
The Machine That Did Nothing

By: Kevin Moore

Copyright © 2021 by Kevin Moore. 828462

All rights reserved. No part of this book may be reproduced
or transmitted in any form or by any means, electronic or
mechanical, including photocopying, recording, or by any
information storage and retrieval system, without permission in
writing from the copyright owner.

This is a work of fiction. Names, characters, places and incidents
either are the product of the author's imagination or are used
fictitiously, and any resemblance to any actual persons, living or
dead, events, or locales is entirely coincidental.

To order additional copies of this book, contact:
Xlibris
844-714-8691
www.Xlibris.com
Orders@Xlibris.com

ISBN: Softcover   978-1-6641-6648-6
         EBook   978-1-6641-6647-9

Print information available on the last page

Rev. date: 03/30/2021

ROAD MAKER ONE

ROAD MAKER ONE

Not yet, but a time to come. Man will invent Road Maker One. With man now being smart as a whip, he's adapted to the ways of the world so quick.

He's created a machine that can chew up the land and lay out a road just as fast as it can. Now man has always had the ability to dream, but this Road Maker takes it to the very extreme. If a man is not careful, he could make a mistake. It could end up costing us the whole human race.

It began as a thought and it grew to be huge, but man didn't know the battle he could lose. It's over one hundred yards long and fifty feet high. It looks like a dinosaur as it slowly goes by.

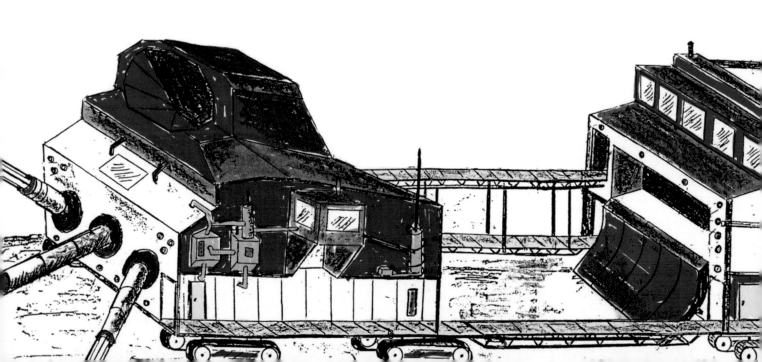

It was made in three parts, but they all worked as one.
It's constructed of steel so it weights eighty tons. It was
designed to help man and built like a train. Each part was
connected and then given a brain.

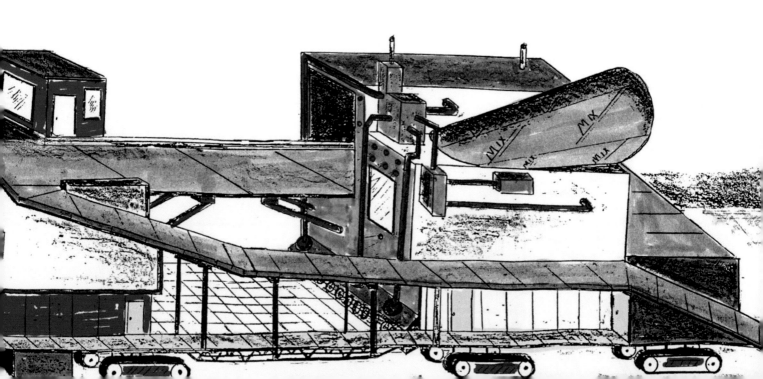

The first of the three is run by Dan. It's job is to simply clear off the land. It can eat a tree whole, pull stumps with great ease. It can do this all day and even collect leaves.

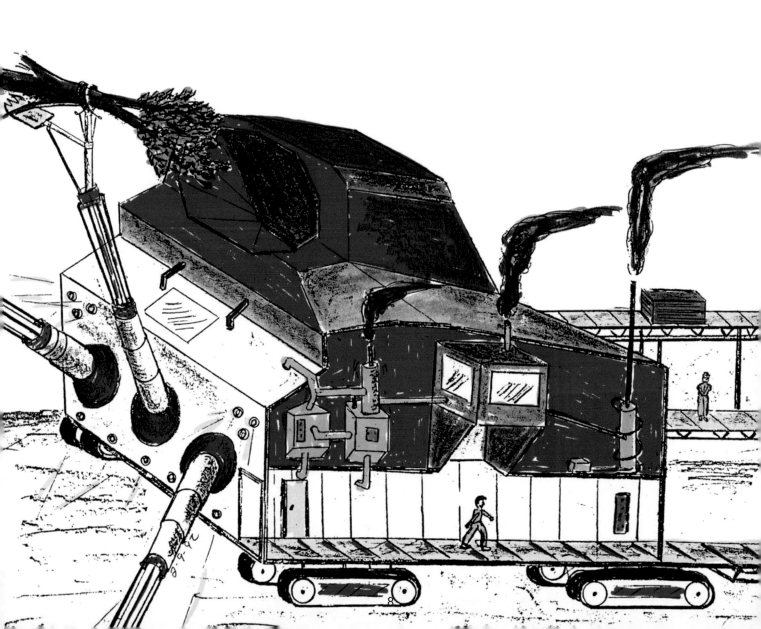

The ground mover comes next, it's second of the three.
It levels off the land just as flat as it could be. It peels back
the top soil and swallows up the dirt. Then it lays the steel
wire down. It's run by a man named Burt.

Last but not least the caboose of this train. It is so advanced
it can work in the rain. It's called the concrete spreader and
it's run by Joe. Surprisingly enough it can work in the snow.

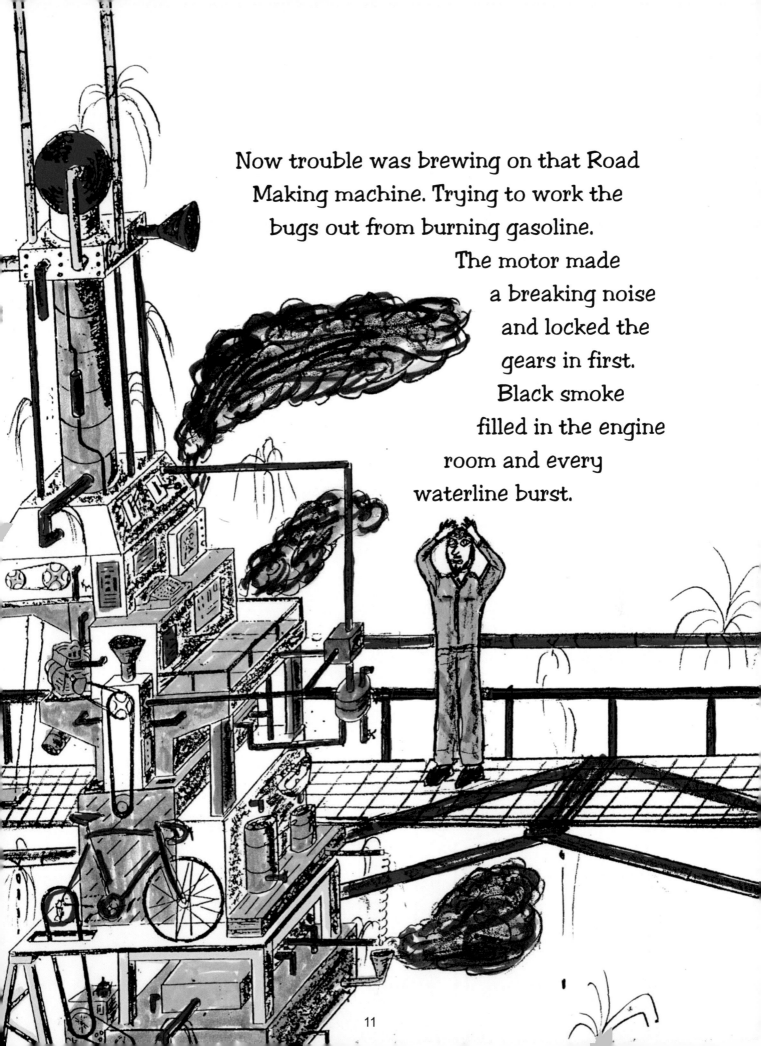

Now trouble was brewing on that Road
Making machine. Trying to work the
bugs out from burning gasoline.
The motor made
a breaking noise
and locked the
gears in first.
Black smoke
filled in the engine
room and every
waterline burst.

Now things were looking bad then suddenly things got worse. That monster machine, it changed it's course. It's like it had a curse. Now Burt, he pulled with all his might to get it out of gear. Then suddenly, the handle broke and everything became quite clear.

This machine seems to have a will of it's own and there is nothing they can do to stop it. This man-made dinosaur is heading west to the last known national forest.

It seems this machine is feeding on trees
and it's swallowing them down like candy.
If something is not done soon we could
lose us the park. So we better call and
warn the Ranger Sandy.

So they called the Ranger and told her what's coming.
She was scared of it's size and felt just like running.
She said, "You know it's my job to protect these trees. I'm asking and pleading on bending knees. Don't let that Road Maker destroy this forest. Stop that runaway dinosauress."

So Joe called a meeting and they studied each option. Their only hope was a new part adoption. So he called up the plant and he told them the story. The plant manager responded saying, "The whole thing sounds gory. We have the solution. It's almost completed. It should solve the problem and totally delete it. We will have it flown as soon as it's finished. Do what you can to get the problem diminished."

So the plant went on overtime and they worked around the clock. It had two overhead cranes and a hundred foot dock. The foreman yelled his orders out and the men went back to work. They knew they had a job to do, in their faith they could not doubt.

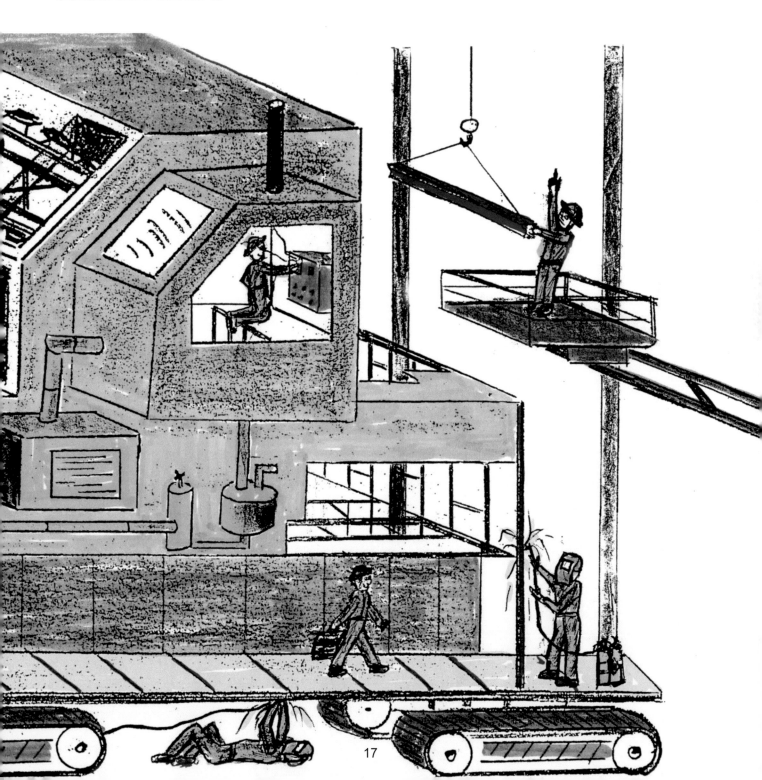

So the crew worked hard and they finished the job. They knew that everyone was waiting. It was all up to them to save those trees and keep the forest from fading. Without air to breathe no one could live and trees have a big part of it. They hoped that man could learn this lesson and never have to repeat it.

Now this unit has a mouth but works like the others. Yet, this one has a different job to do. This fourth part is a digger and loves to make tunnels. To man, it was definitely brand new. The foreman gave a great big thanks as they carried it out the door. This extra machine would go in the front, the Road Maker would then number four.

Meanwhile, back at Road Maker One, they tried everything to stop it. That monster machine had entered in the starting of the national forest. One after one it swallowed trees down. With a path of destruction behind it. Could this be the end of life on earth? Or can man be quick to out smart it?

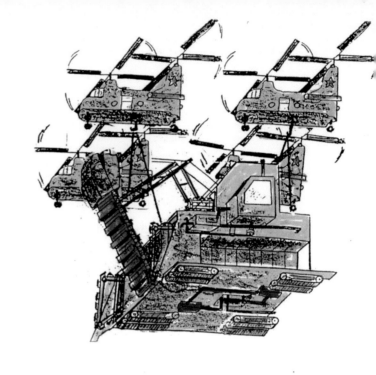

When over their heads high in the sky, it was coming to save the day. They were happy to see it and hoped it would work as four helicopters carried it their way.

It flew right over the top of road Maker One. The men all cheered at its arrival. It was gently set down then connected together. They had to work fast for man's survival.

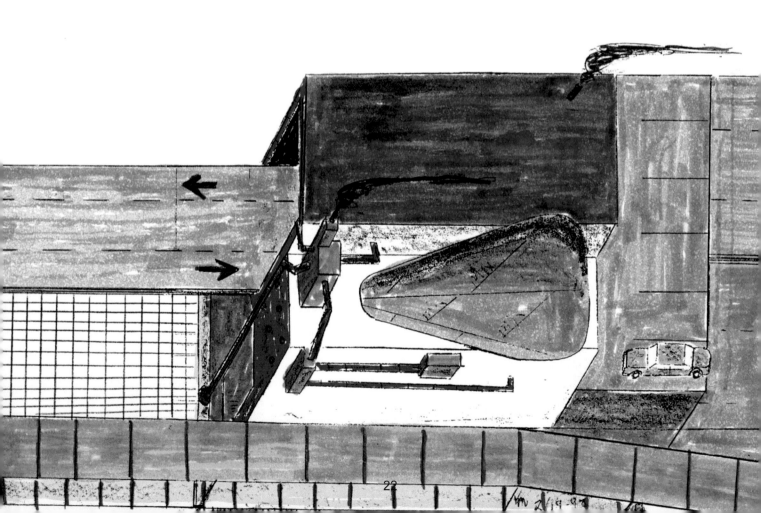

So they turned on the engine and it worked just great, the world now had a reason to celebrate. But the job wasn't finished, they had a long way to go. They had to dig a tunnel under the forest, you know.

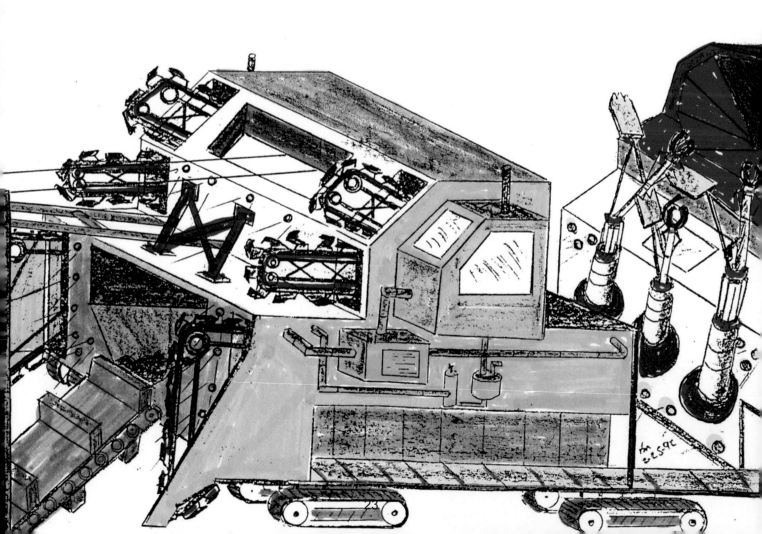

So Tim put it in great and away it went. That machine ate dirt just like it was meant. The world danced for joy because the trees were all saved and that tunnel would make history as the first man-made cave.

All of mankind took a sigh of relief as it went underground about fifty-three feet. So the forest was safe and the road still went through. My hats off to man and what he can prove. For what is it worth to have all of man's smarts. If no one is around to enjoy a national park.

The Machine That Did Nothing

THE MACHINE THAT DID NOTHING

Once upon a time, there lived a man names Art. Now, Art loved to make things. One day, while cleaning out his garage, Art got a wonderful idea he called Monterage. Instead of throwing all his old stuff away, he would make something grand in his backyard that day. So he loaded his wagon with all it could hold and he started that thing that dared not to be sold.

So, Art pushed out a load and then he pushed two. He cleaned out his garage right down to his shoes. Art piled it up as high as he could. Then he started to build what he thought that he should.

Art put in a plug and he screwed in a tube. He welded and soldered and hammered a few. He took a step back and it wasn't quite right. So, he added a sink and a red ten speed bike.

Art built on that thing all day in the sun. He put in a swing and had lots of fun. He used an old vacuum, the TV and some. Art used his son's mini-bike and two fifty-five gallon drums.

Art climbed up his
ladder and he got on
the top. He added blue
buttons, he just could not
stop. He built that thing up to
about forty feet tall and finished
it off with a big purple ball.

33

He climbed down the side and he said, "That is that. It looks like it's finished. I'll show my wife Pat." Art ran in the house, his heart set on fire, excited to tell about the thing he conspired.

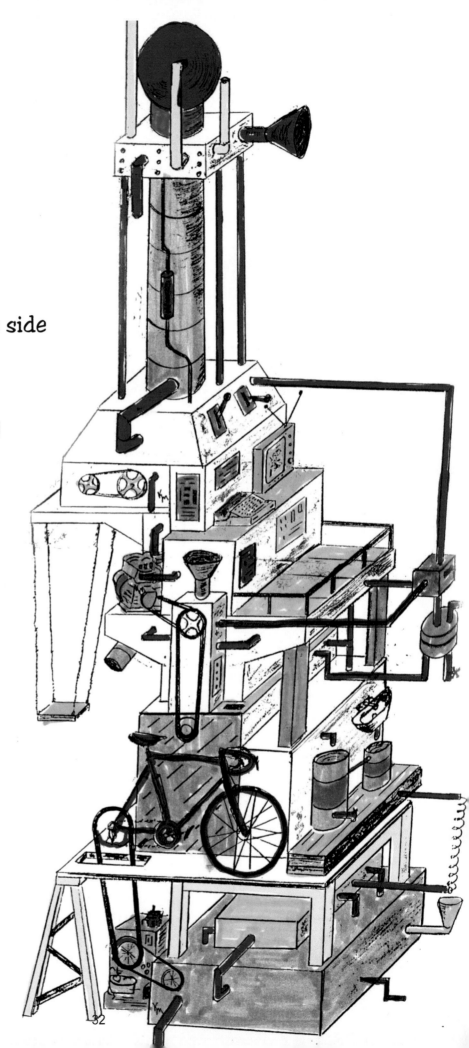

Art said with great joy, "Oh, honey come see. This thing I have built for you and for me." Pat ran to the window, threw open the curtain. Her teeth fell out, her eye started hurting. She stared out the window. Orange smoke filled her head. Red fire in her eyes, she turned and she said, "You built what in our yard? Oh this I can see. Please take it away immediately."

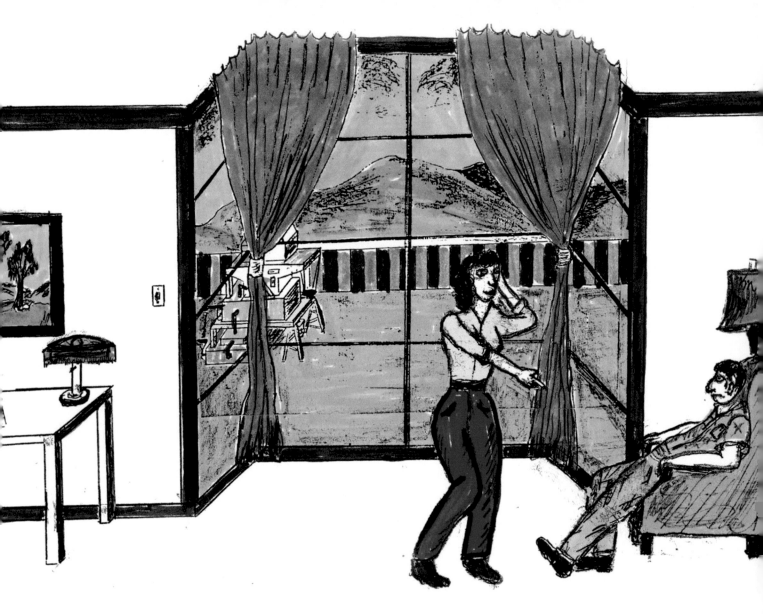

Art was sad to think his wife could not see, that thing he had made for you and me. He thought for a moment and whispered in Pat's ear, "I cannot destroy this thing my dear." Pat nodded her head and said with great pain, "I see that you are serious and not quite insane, but this thing can't stay in our backyard, you see. For what would the neighbors surely think of me."

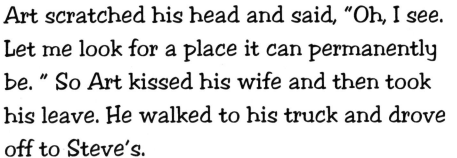

Art scratched his head and said, "Oh, I see. Let me look for a place it can permanently be. " So Art kissed his wife and then took his leave. He walked to his truck and drove off to Steve's.

Now mean Lady Hawkins who lived down the way, was walking her dog that very same day. When she got down to Art's house she looked up to see, that forty foot tower as tall as could be. She ran to the door and started knocking away. "There has to be an ordinance against that, I say. I'm calling the police, you just wait and see. They will smash it to the ground and it will no longer be."

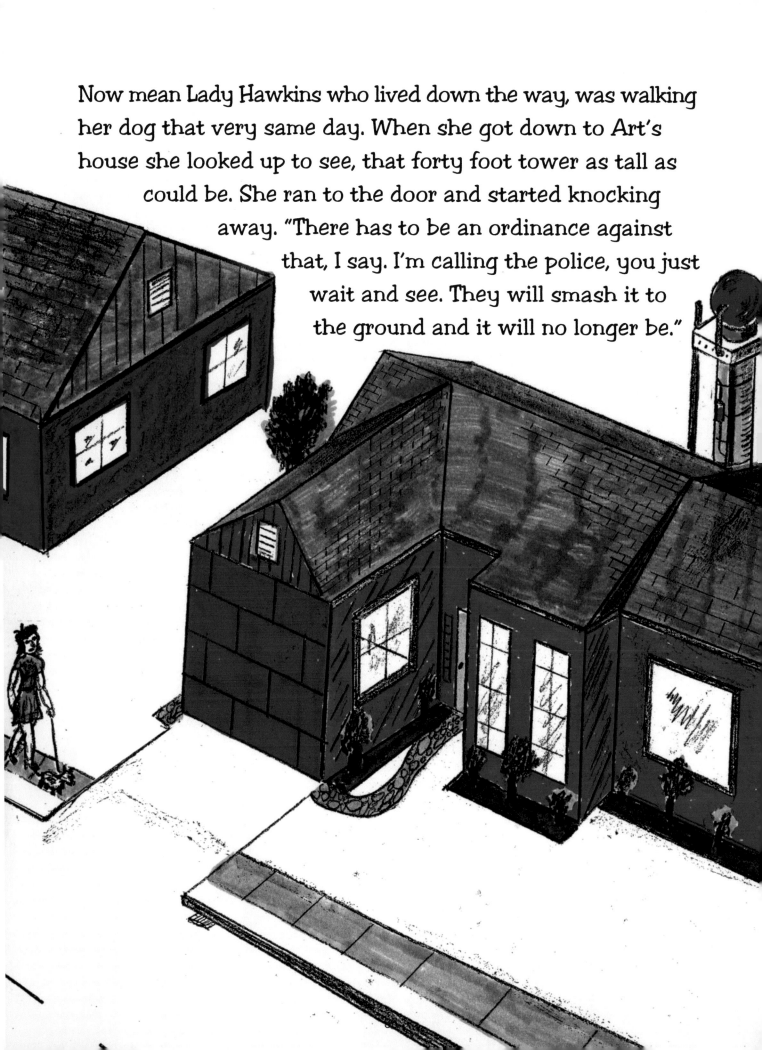

Now Pat was embarrassed to open the door. She hid in some clothes piled up on her floor. The cats out of the bag, it's a shame she couldn't see. This one of a kind thing that was meant to be. So mean Lady Hawkins went straight home to call. She told the police exactly what she saw. The police said, "Don't move. We have a car on the way. We'll have it torn down by the end of the day."

The police got to Art's house and radioed in to say, "You would not believe it. Send help right away. That lady was right, it stands fifty feet tall. We're not sure what it does. Stand by, we'll call." So the police jumped out to investigate the trouble. When Mean Lady Hawkins came running on the double. She said, "I'm the one who called in the complaint. Come see for yourself, it still has wet paint."

They called in a helicopter for an aerial view. The pilot reported, "That thing is huge. From here it looks like a rocket or maybe a bomb? You better call the fire department, they will keep things calm."

So they called on old fire engine number sixty-nine. It arrived at Art's house in the nick of time. The bomb squad pulled up and parked right along side. They were there to make sure that no one died.

The Police Chief took charge and blocked off the street.
The Fire Truck got ready just in case there was heat.
The Bomb Squad went in decked out in fire suits,
they were protected from danger right
down to their boots.

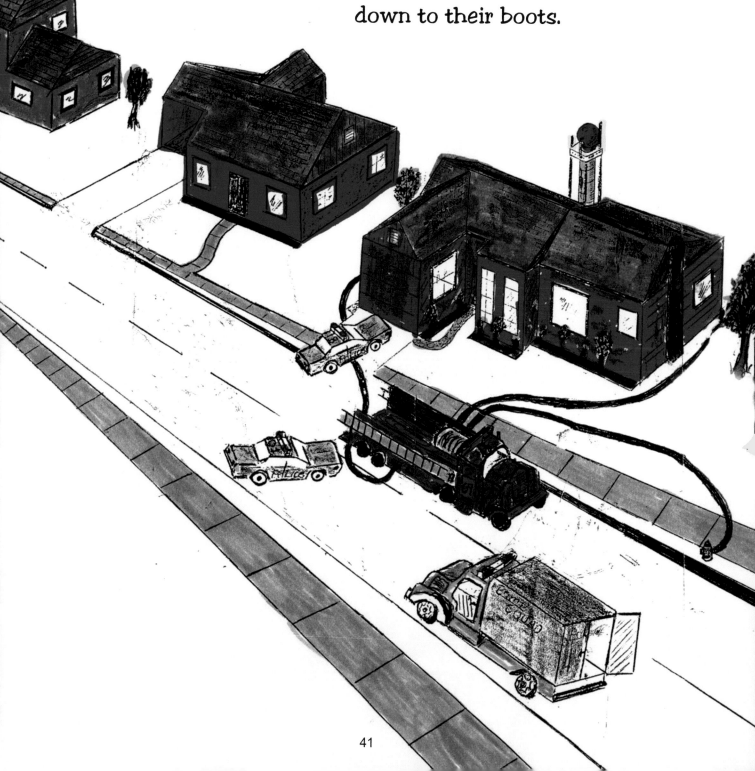

They examined that thing and went over it twice. They looked in the sink, they looked down the pipes. The Captain stood up and spoke with great boast, "This isn't a bomb, it's not even close." The Chief scratched his head and said, "What could it be? I know it's not a bomb that I can see. So figure it out and don't tell me you can't. It could be a nuclear power plant."

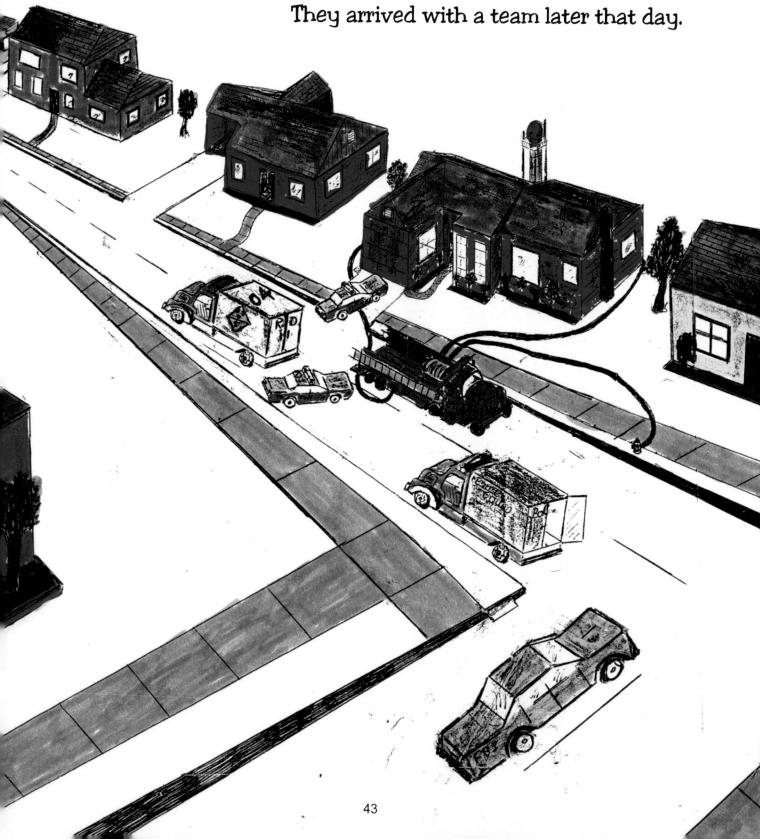

So they scrambled around and they called up the Feds.
The Chief told them the story off the top of his head. The
F.B.I. thought that it was, so they came right away.
They arrived with a team later that day.

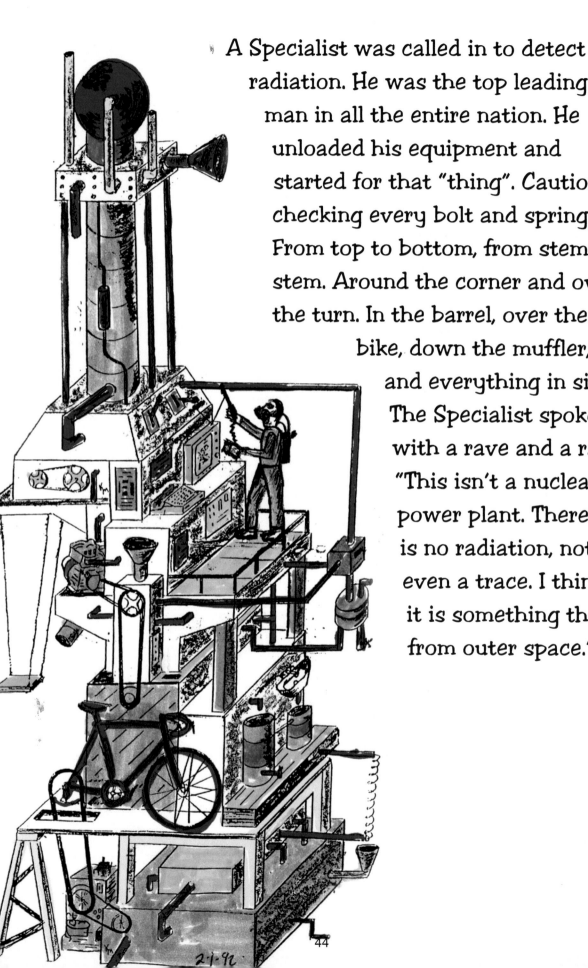

A Specialist was called in to detect radiation. He was the top leading man in all the entire nation. He unloaded his equipment and started for that "thing". Cautiously checking every bolt and spring. From top to bottom, from stem to stem. Around the corner and over the turn. In the barrel, over the bike, down the muffler, and everything in sight. The Specialist spoke up with a rave and a rant, "This isn't a nuclear power plant. There is no radiation, not even a trace. I think it is something that's from outer space."

Now that stirred up trouble, enough for a war.
They called up the President and told him the score.
They called in three Scientist and the C.I.A . . . They brought
with them a crane to take it away. The Media found out and
set up their camp; TV, Radio and Newspaper Scamps.
They blew up the story, like never before.
If only Art was there to tell
them what for.

Now Art found a place it could permanently stay.
When he turned down his street late in that day. Art
stopped his truck and said with concern,
"I really don't think these people
will learn!"

Art walked to his house and then in the back.
When mean Lady Hawkins said, "There is that maniac!"
Art was quickly surrounded as he said, "Let me explain,
I take full responsibility. I am not crazy or insane."

"That thing I had made is not a machine. It doesn't do anything but give hope and good dreams. It's nothing but a statue. It comes from my heart. It's better known to you as a work of Art."

The End

Printed in the United States
by Baker & Taylor Publisher Services